To my husband and children for their love and support,
and to Nomi for bringing light and joy into every day.

CIP data for this book is available from the Library of Congress.

Published by Creston Books, LLC
www.crestonbooks.co

Source of Production: Worzalla Books, Stevens Point, Wisconsin
Printed and bound in the United States of America

1 2 3 4 5

FSC
www.fsc.org
MIX
Paper from
responsible sources
FSC® C002589

Lola Goes To The Doctor

Creston Books

Today I am going to visit my doctor.

I am a little nervous.
Maybe even a teeny tiny bit afraid.

I don't know why,
because the waiting room has nice toys.

And there are usually interesting animals.
I wonder how you give a chicken a checkup.

Or a pig?

Sometimes I see the doctor when I am sick,
but today I am getting my regular checkup.

I try to wait patiently,
just like the big dog.

Finally the nurse calls my name and takes me into a special room.
I'm scared, but I tell myself I'm a big dog, too.

The doctor comes in and says, "Hello, how are you?"
His voice is soft and kind.

First, I get on the scale, and we find out how much I weigh.
When will I ever get bigger?

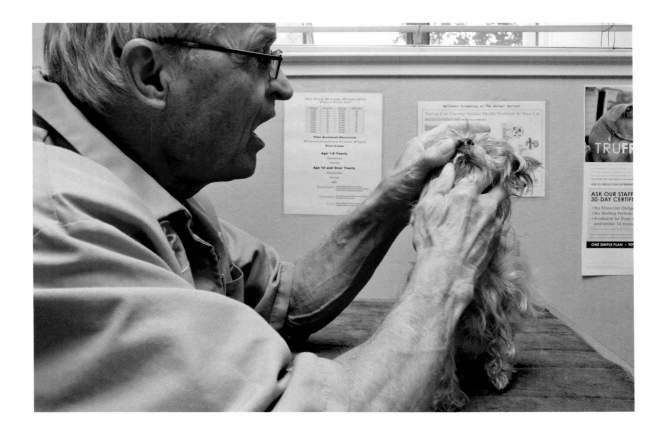

The doctor is very gentle when he looks at my teeth.

And when he checks my neck and throat.

I don't really like it when he takes my temperature.

Or looks in my ears.
But I try to stay very still.

I'm not afraid when he uses his stethoscope to listen to my lungs.

It kind of tickles when he listens to my heart.

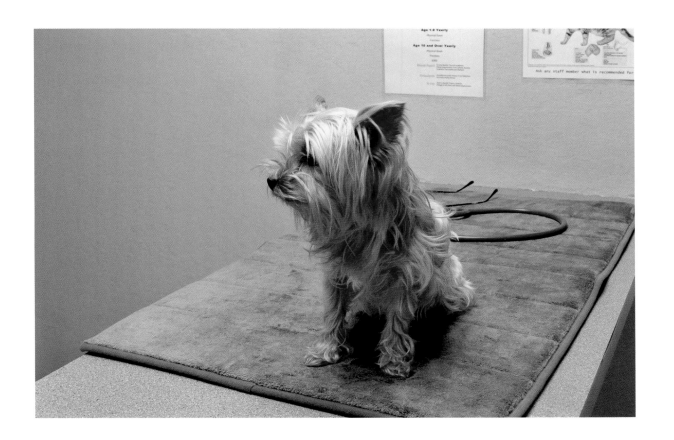

Uh oh! I think it might be time for my shot!

Now I remember why I was nervous,
even a tiny bit scared!

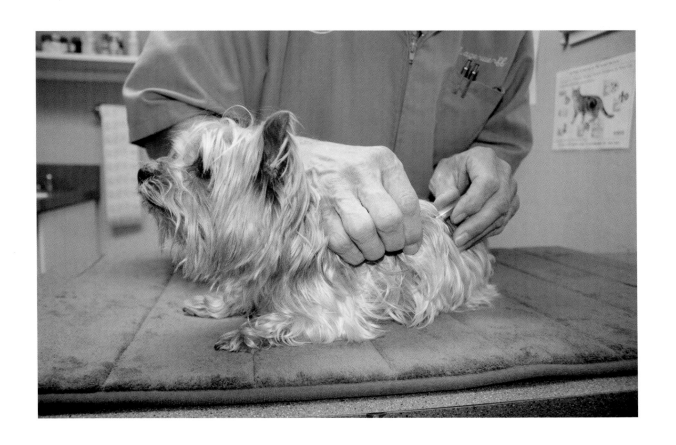

But I'm a big dog...

It stings a bit, but I am very brave.

When my exam is over,
my doctor says that I am very healthy.

He gives me a treat for being so good!

I wonder how the doctor gives a shot to the snake?

Or to the goldfish?

I wonder who I'll see in the waiting room next time.

I'll come back to see the doctor next year.
I bet I'll be bigger and braver then!

Curriculum Guide

Focus Words:
-Discuss the meaning of words and/or role-play the meaning of words; what are other situations where we may experience these feelings or have to practice these behaviors?
•Nervous •Patient •Afraid •Brave

Questions:
-Why did Lola visit the doctor? How can you take care of yourself to stay healthy?
-Where did the doctor use a stethoscope to listen to Lola's body? Where is your heart? What do your lungs do?
-Name the other parts of Lola that the doctor checked. Locate these parts on your own body
(add other body parts to be located – making it more complicated depending on the skill level of the child).
-Why did the doctor give Lola a shot? What kind of shots do you get?
-Are there some other reasons you might go to the doctor's office? How can a doctor help you?
-Has a doctor ever made you feel better? How?
-Why was Lola nervous? Patient? Afraid? Brave? How did she act when she felt these things?
-What makes you feel nervous or patient, afraid or brave?

Activities:
-Use a doctor's tool kit to role-play a visit to the doctor. Use stuffed animals, dolls, puppets, or cutouts as the patient (draw your own or have the child color an already-made cutout).
-Act out the focus words above and further discuss what to do to take care of ourselves and be safe.
-Draw parts of your body that the doctor checks when you go for a visit. Do you stick out your tongue?
-Does the doctor check your teeth the way he does for Lola?